RAINBOW magic

RAINBOW FAIRIES

RUBY
THE RED FAIRY

By Daisy Meadows
Illustrated by Georgie Ripper

Silver Dolphin

Silver Dolphin Books
An imprint of Printers Row Publishing Group
A division of Readerlink Distribution Services, LLC
9717 Pacific Heights Blvd, San Diego, CA 92121
www.silverdolphinbooks.com

Printers Row Publishing Group is a division of
Readerlink Distribution Services, LLC.
Silver Dolphin Books is a registered trademark of
Readerlink Distribution Services, LLC.

All notations of errors or omissions should be addressed to Silver
Dolphin Books, Editorial Department, at the above address. All other
correspondence (author inquiries, permissions) concerning the
content of this book should be addressed to:
Hachette Children's Group
Carmelite House
50 Victoria Embankment
London
EC4Y 0DZ

ISBN: 978-1-6672-0434-5
Manufactured, printed, and assembled in Pittston, PA, USA.
First printing, February 2023. KA/02/23
27 26 25 24 23   1 2 3 4 5

The Fairyland Palace

Maze

Forest

Orchard

Black Pot

Meadow

Tower

Beach

Tide pools

Rainspell Island

Cold winds blow and thick ice form,
I conjure up this fairy storm.
To seven corners of the human world
the Rainbow Fairies will be hurled!

I curse every part of Fairyland,
with a frosty wave of my icy hand.
For now and always, from this day,
Fairyland will be cold and gray!

Table of Contents

THE END OF THE RAINBOW

"Look, Dad!" said Rachel Walker. She pointed across the blue-green sea at the rocky island ahead of them. The ferry was sailing toward it, dipping up and down on the rolling waves. "Is that Rainspell Island?" she asked.

Her dad nodded. "Yes, it is," he said, smiling. "Our vacation is about to begin!"

The waves slapped against the side
of the ferry as it bobbed up and down on
the water. Rachel felt her heart thump with
excitement. She could see white cliffs and
emerald-green fields on the island. And
golden sandy beaches, with tide pools here
and there.

Suddenly, a few raindrops plopped down
on Rachel's head. "Oh!" she gasped,
surprised. The sun was still shining.

Rachel's mom grabbed her hand. "Let's get under cover," she said, leading Rachel inside.

"Isn't that strange?" Rachel said. "Sunshine *and* rain!"

"Let's hope the rain stops before we get off the ferry," said Mr. Walker. "Now, where did I put that map of the island?"

Rachel looked out of the window. Her eyes opened wide.

A girl was standing alone on the deck. Her dark hair was wet with raindrops, but she didn't seem to care. She just stared up at the sky.

Rachel looked over at her mom and dad. They were busy studying the map. So Rachel slipped back outside to see what was so interesting.

And there it was.

In the blue sky, high above them, was the most amazing rainbow that Rachel had ever seen. One end of the rainbow stretched far out to sea. The other seemed to fall somewhere on Rainspell Island. All of the colors were bright and clear.

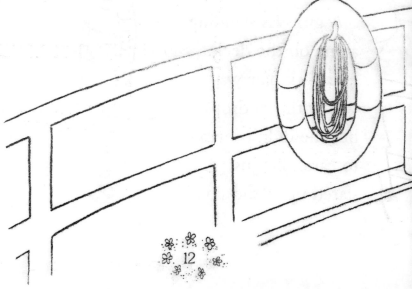

Red
Orange
Yellow
Green
Blue
Indigo
Violet

"Isn't it perfect?" the dark-haired girl whispered to Rachel.

"Yes, it is," Rachel agreed. "Are you going to Rainspell on vacation?"

The girl nodded. "We're staying for a week," she said. "I'm Kirsty Tate."

Rachel smiled as the rain began to stop. "I'm Rachel Walker. We're staying at Mermaid Cottage," she added.

"Oh! We're at Dolphin Cottage," said Kirsty. "Do you think we might be close to each other?"

"I hope so," Rachel replied. She had a feeling she was going to like Kirsty.

Kirsty leaned over the rail and looked down into the shimmering water. "The ocean looks really deep here, doesn't it?" she said. "There might even be mermaids down there, watching us right now!"

Rachel stared at the waves. She saw something that made her heart skip a beat. "Look!" she said. "Is that a mermaid's hair?" Then she laughed when she saw that it was just seaweed.

"It could be a mermaid's necklace," said Kirsty, smiling. "Maybe she lost it when she was trying to escape from a sea monster."

The ferry was now sailing
into Rainspell's tiny
harbor. Seagulls flew
around them, and
fishing boats bobbed
on the water.
"Look at that
big white cliff over
there," Kirsty said.
She pointed it out
to Rachel.
"It looks like
a giant's face,
doesn't it?"
Rachel
looked, and
nodded. Kirsty
seemed to see
magic *everywhere*.

"There you are, Rachel!" called Mrs. Walker. Rachel turned around and saw her mom and dad coming out onto the deck. "We'll be getting off the ferry in a few minutes," Mrs. Walker added.

"Mom, Dad, this is Kirsty," Rachel said. "She's staying at Dolphin Cottage."

"That's right next door to ours," said Mr. Walker. "I remember seeing it on the map."

Rachel and Kirsty looked at each other and smiled.

"I'd better go and find *my* mom and dad," said Kirsty. She looked around. "Oh, there they are."

Kirsty's mom and dad came over to
say hello to the Walkers. Then the ferry
docked, and everyone began to leave
the boat.

"Our cottages are on the other side of
the harbor," said Rachel's dad, looking at
the map. "It's not too far."

Mermaid Cottage and Dolphin Cottage
were right next to the beach. Rachel loved
her bedroom, which was high up in the
attic. From the window, she could see the
waves rolling onto the sand.

A shout from outside made Rachel look down. It was Kirsty. She was standing under the window, waving.

"Let's go and explore the beach!" Kirsty called.

Rachel dashed outside to join her.

Piles of seaweed lay on the sand, and there were tiny pink-and-white shells sprinkled everywhere.

"I love it here already!" Rachel shouted happily above the noise of the seagulls.

"Me too," Kirsty said. She pointed up at the sky. "Look, the rainbow's still there."

Rachel looked up. The rainbow glowed brightly among the fluffy white clouds.

"Have you heard the story about the pot of gold at the end of the rainbow?" Kirsty asked.

Rachel nodded. "Yes, but that's just in fairy tales," she said.

Kirsty grinned. "Maybe. But let's go and find out for ourselves!"

"OK," Rachel agreed. "And maybe we can explore the island at the same time."

They rushed back to tell their parents where they were going. Then Kirsty and Rachel set off along a road behind the cottages. It led them away from the beach, across green fields, and toward a small stretch of woods.

Rachel kept looking up at the rainbow. She was worried that it would start to fade now that the rain had stopped. But the colors stayed clear and bright.

"It looks like the end of the rainbow is over there," Kirsty said. "Come on!" And she hurried toward the trees.

The woods were cool and shady after being in the heat of the sun. Rachel and Kirsty followed a winding path until they came to a clearing. Then they both stopped and stared.

The rainbow shone down onto the grass through a gap in the trees. Its colors sparkled and twinkled brightly.

And there, at the rainbow's end, lay an old, black pot.

A TINY SURPRISE

"Look!" Kirsty whispered. "There really *is* a pot of gold!"

"It could just be a cooking pot," Rachel said doubtfully. "Some campers might have left it behind."

But Kirsty shook her head. "I don't think so," she said. "It looks really old."

Rachel stared at the pot. It was sitting on the grass, upside down.

"Let's have a closer look," said Kirsty. She ran to the pot and tried to turn it over. "Oh, it's heavy!" she gasped. She tried again, but the pot didn't move.

Rachel rushed to help her. They both pushed and pushed at the pot. This time it moved, but just a little.

"Let's try again," Kirsty panted. "Are you ready, Rachel?"

Tap! Tap! Tap!

Rachel and Kirsty stared at each other.

"What was that?" Rachel gasped.

"I don't know," whispered Kirsty.

Tap! Tap!

"There it is again," Kirsty said. She looked down at the pot lying on the grass. "You know what? I think it's coming from inside this pot!"

Rachel's eyes opened wide. "Are you sure?" She bent down, and put her ear to the pot. *Tap! Tap!* Then, to her amazement, Rachel heard a tiny voice.

"Help!" it called. "Help me!"

Rachel grabbed Kirsty's arm. "Did you hear that?" she asked.

Kirsty nodded. "Quick!" she said. "We have to turn the pot over, somehow!"

Rachel and Kirsty pushed at the pot as hard as they could. It began to rock from side to side on the grass.

"We're almost there!" Rachel cried. "Keep pushing, Kirsty!"

The girls pushed with all their might. Suddenly, the pot turned over and rolled onto its side. Rachel and Kirsty were taken by surprise. They both lost their balance and landed on the grass with a thump.

"Look!" Kirsty whispered, breathing hard.

A small shower of sparkling red dust had flown out of the pot. Rachel and Kirsty gasped with surprise. The dust hung in the air above them. And there, right in the middle of the glittering cloud, was a tiny, winged girl.

Rachel and Kirsty watched in wonder as the tiny girl fluttered in the sunlight. Her delicate wings sparkled with all the colors of the rainbow.

"Oh, Rachel!" Kirsty whispered. "It's a fairy . . ."

FAIRY MAGIC

The fairy flew over Rachel and Kirsty's
heads. Her short, silky dress was the color
of ripe strawberries. Red crystal earrings
glowed in her ears. Her golden hair was
braided with tiny red roses, and she wore
crimson slippers on her little feet.

The fairy waved her scarlet wand,
and a shower of sparkling red fairy dust
floated softly down to the ground. Where
the dust landed, all kinds of red flowers
appeared with a *pop*!

Rachel and Kirsty watched open
mouthed. This really and truly *was* a fairy.

"This is like a dream," Rachel said.

"I always believed in fairies," Kirsty
whispered back. "But I never thought I'd
ever *see* one!"

The fairy flew toward them. "Oh,
thank you *so* much!" she called in a tiny
voice. "I'm free at last!" She glided down
and landed on Kirsty's hand.

Kirsty gasped. The fairy felt lighter and
softer than a butterfly.

"I was beginning to think I'd *never* get
out of the pot!" the fairy said.

Kirsty wanted to ask the fairy so many things. But she didn't know where to start.

"Tell me your names, quickly," said the fairy. She fluttered up into the air again. "There's so much to be done, and we must get started right away."

Rachel wondered what the fairy meant. "I'm Rachel," she said.

"And I'm Kirsty," said Kirsty. "But who are *you*?"

"I'm the Red Rainbow Fairy—but you can call me Ruby," the fairy replied.

"Ruby. . . " Kirsty breathed. "A Rainbow Fairy. . . " She and Rachel stared at each other in excitement. This really *was* magic!

"Yes," said Ruby. "And I have six sisters: Amber, Sunny, Fern, Sky, Inky, and Heather. One for each color of the rainbow, you see."

"What do Rainbow Fairies do?"
Rachel asked.

Ruby flew over and landed lightly
on Rachel's hand. "It's our job to put
all the different colors into Fairyland,"
she explained.

"So why were you trapped under
that old pot?" asked Rachel.

"And where are your sisters?"
Kirsty added.

Ruby's golden wings drooped. Her
eyes filled with tiny, sparkling tears.
"I don't know," she said. "Something
terrible has happened in Fairyland.
We *really* need your help!"

FAIRIES IN DANGER

Kirsty stared down at Ruby, sitting sadly on Rachel's hand. "Of course we'll help you!" she said.

"Just tell us how," added Rachel.

Ruby wiped the tears from her eyes. "Thank you!" she said. "But first I must show you the terrible thing that has happened. Follow me—as quickly as you can!"

She flew into the air,
her wings shimmering in
the sunshine.

Rachel and Kirsty
followed Ruby
across the clearing.
The fairy danced
ahead of them,
glowing like a
crimson flame.
She stopped at
a small pond
under a weeping
willow tree. "Look!
I can *show* you what
happened yesterday," she
said. Ruby flew over the
pond and scattered another shower
of sparkling fairy dust with her tiny,
red wand.

All at once, the water lit up with a strange, silver light. It bubbled and fizzed, and then became still. With wide eyes, Rachel and Kirsty watched as a picture appeared in the water. It was like looking through a window into another land!

"Oh, Rachel, look!" said Kirsty.

A river of the brightest blue ran swiftly past hills of the greenest green. Scattered on the hillsides were red-and-white toadstool houses.

And on top of the highest hill stood a silver palace with four pink towers.

The towers were so high, their points were almost hidden by the fluffy white clouds that floated past.

Hundreds of fairies were making their way toward the palace. Some were walking and some were flying. Rachel and Kirsty could see goblins, elves, and pixies too. Everyone seemed very excited.

"Yesterday was the day of the Fairyland Midsummer Ball," Ruby explained. She flew over the pond and pointed with her wand at a spot in the middle of the scene. "There I am, with my Rainbow sisters."

Kirsty and Rachel looked closely at where Ruby was pointing. They saw seven fairies, each dressed prettily in their own rainbow color. Wherever they flew,

they left a trail of fairy dust behind them.

"The Midsummer Ball is *very* special,"
Ruby went on. "And my sisters and I are
always in charge of sending out invitations."

The front doors of the palace slowly opened to the sound of tinkling music.

"Here come King Oberon and Queen Titania," said Ruby. "The Fairy King and Queen. They are about to begin the ball."

Kirsty and Rachel watched as the king and queen stepped through the doors. The king wore a splendid golden coat and crown. His queen wore a silver

dress and a tiara that sparkled with diamonds.

Everyone cheered loudly. After a while, the king signaled for quiet. "Fairies and friends," he began. "We are very

glad to see you all here. Welcome to the
Midsummer Ball!"

The fairies clapped their hands and cheered
again. A band of green frogs in purple suits
started to play their instruments, and the
dancing began.

Suddenly, a gray mist filled the room.
Kirsty and Rachel watched in alarm as all the
fairies started to shiver.

Then a loud, chilly voice shouted out,
"Stop the music!"

The band fell silent. Everyone looked
scared. A tall, bony figure was pushing his
way through the crowd. He was dressed all
in white, and there were tiny icicles on his
white hair and beard. But his face
was red and angry.

"Who's that?" Rachel asked with a shiver. Ice had begun to form around the edge of the pond.

"It's Jack Frost," said Ruby. And she shivered, too.

In the watery picture Jack Frost glared at the seven Rainbow Fairies. "Why wasn't I invited to the Midsummer Ball?" he asked coldly.

The Rainbow Fairies gasped in horror . . .

Ruby looked up and smiled sadly at Rachel and Kirsty. "Yes, we forgot to invite Jack Frost," she said, and looked back at the pond.

They watched as the Fairy Queen stepped forward. "You are more than welcome, Jack Frost," she said. "Please stay and enjoy the ball."

But Jack Frost looked even more angry.
"Too late!" he hissed. "You forgot to
invite me!" He turned and pointed a
thin, icy finger at the Rainbow Fairies.

"Well, you will not forget this!" he went
on. "My spell will banish the Rainbow
Fairies to the seven corners of the human
world. From this day on, Fairyland will be
without color—forever!"

JACK FROST'S SPELL

As Rachel and Kirsty kept watching the pond's surface, they saw Jack Frost cast his spell. A great, icy wind began to blow. It picked up the seven Rainbow Fairies and spun them up into the darkening sky. The other fairies could only watch in dismay.

Jack Frost turned to the king and queen. "Your Rainbow Fairies will be trapped, far away. They will be all alone, and they will never return." With that, he left, leaving only a trail of icy footprints behind.

Quickly, the Fairy Queen stepped forward and lifted her silver wand. "Jack Frost's magic is very powerful. I cannot undo it completely," she shouted, as the wind howled and rushed around her. "But I can guide the Rainbow Fairies to a place where they will be safe **until they are rescued!**"

The queen pointed her wand at the gray sky overhead. A black pot came spinning through the stormy clouds. It flew toward the Rainbow Fairies. One by one, the Rainbow Fairies tumbled into the pot.

"May this pot at the end of the rainbow keep our Rainbow Fairies together and safe," the queen called. "And take them to Rainspell Island!"

As Rachel, Kirsty, and Ruby watched, the pot flew out of sight. It disappeared behind a dark cloud. And the bright colors of Fairyland began to fade, until the beautiful land looked like an old black-and-white photograph.

"Oh no!" Kirsty gasped. "All the color is gone." Then the picture in the pond vanished.

"So the Fairy Queen cast her *own* spell!" Rachel said. She was bursting with questions. "She put you and your sisters in the pot, and sent you to Rainspell Island?"

Ruby nodded. "Our queen knew that we would be safe here," she said. "We know Rainspell well. It is a place full of magic."

"But where are your sisters?" Kirsty

asked. "They were in the pot, too."

Ruby looked upset. "Jack Frost's magic was very strong," she said. "The wind from his spell blew my sisters right out of the pot. We were still spinning through the sky, and all at once they were gone." Ruby shook her head. "I was at the bottom, so I was safe. But I was trapped when the pot landed upside down. In the dark, I was frightened and alone. My fairy magic wouldn't even work!"

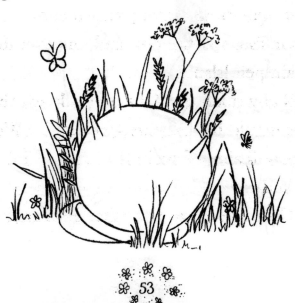

"So are your sisters somewhere on Rainspell?" Kirsty asked.

Ruby nodded. "Yes, but they're scattered all over the island. I'm sure Jack Frost's spell has trapped them, too." She flew toward Kirsty and landed on her shoulder. "That's where you and Rachel come in."

"How?" Rachel asked.

"You found *me*, didn't you?" the fairy went on. "That's because you believe in magic." She flew from Kirsty's shoulder to Rachel's. "So, you could rescue my Rainbow sisters, too! Once we're together, we can bring color back to Fairyland again."

A VISIT TO FAIRYLAND

"Of course we'll search for your sisters,"
Kirsty said quickly. "Won't we, Rachel?"
Rachel nodded.

"Oh, thank you," Ruby said happily.

"But we're only here for a week,"
Rachel said. "Will that be long enough?"

"We must get started right away,"
said Ruby. "First, I must take you to

Fairyland to meet our king and queen.
They will be very pleased to know
that you are going to help me find my
sisters."

Rachel and Kirsty stared at Ruby.

"You're taking us to *Fairyland*?" Kirsty
gasped. She could hardly believe her ears.

"But how will we get there?" Rachel
wanted to know.

"We'll fly," Ruby replied.

"But *we* can't fly!" Rachel pointed out.

Ruby smiled. She whirled up into
the air over the girls' heads. Then she
swirled her wand above them. Magic red
fairy dust fluttered down.

Rachel and Kirsty began to feel a bit
strange. Were the trees getting bigger or
were they getting smaller?

They were getting *smaller*! Rachel and Kirsty got smaller and smaller, until they were the same size as Ruby.

"I'm tiny!" Rachel laughed. She was so small, the flowers around her seemed as big as trees.

Kirsty twisted around to look at her back. She had wings—shiny and delicate as a butterfly's! Ruby beamed at them. "Now you can fly," she said. "Let's go."

Rachel twitched her shoulders. Her wings fluttered, and she rose up into the air. She felt very wobbly at first. Flying was not at all like walking!

"Help!" Kirsty yelled, as she shot up into the air. "I'm not very good at this!"

"Come on," said Ruby, taking their hands. "I'll help you." She led them up, out of the meadow.

From the air, Rachel looked down on Rainspell Island. She could see the cottages next to the beach, and the harbor.

"Where *is* Fairyland, Ruby?" Kirsty asked. They were flying higher and higher, up into the clouds.

"It's so far away that no human could ever find it," Ruby said.

They flew on through the clouds for a long, long time. But at last Ruby turned to them and smiled. "We're here," she said. "Luckily, while we're in Fairyland, no time passes in your world. No one will even know you were gone!"

As they flew down from the clouds, Kirsty and Rachel saw places they recognized from the pond picture: the palace, the hillsides with their toadstool houses, and the river. But there were no bright colors now. Because of Jack Frost's spell, everything was a drab shade of gray.

A few fairies walked miserably across the hillsides. Their wings hung limply down their backs.

No one even had the energy to fly.

Suddenly, one of the fairies glanced up into the sky. "Look!" she shouted. "It's Ruby. She's come back!"

At once, the fairies flew up toward Ruby, Kirsty, and Rachel.

They circled around Ruby, looking
much happier, and asking lots of questions.

"Where are the other Rainbow Fairies?"
"Who are your friends?"
"First, we must see the king and queen.
Then I will tell you everything!" Ruby
promised.

King Oberon and Queen Titania were
seated on their thrones. Their palace was

as gray and gloomy as everywhere else in Fairyland. But they smiled warmly when Ruby arrived with Rachel and Kirsty.

"Welcome back, Ruby," the queen said. "We have missed you."

"Your Majesties, I have found two humans who believe in magic!" Ruby announced. "These are my friends, Kirsty and Rachel."

Quickly, Ruby explained what had happened to the other Rainbow Fairies. She told everyone how Rachel and Kirsty had rescued her.

"You have our thanks," the king told them. "Our Rainbow Fairies are very special to us."

"And will you help us find Ruby's Rainbow sisters?" the queen asked.

"Yes, we will," Kirsty said.

"But how will we know where to look?" Rachel asked.

"The trick is not to look too hard," said Queen Titania. "Don't worry. As you enjoy the rest of your vacation, the magic you need to find each Rainbow Fairy will find *you*. Just wait and see."

King Oberon rubbed his beard thoughtfully. "You have six days of your vacation left, and six fairies to find," he said. "A fairy each day. That's a lot of fairy-finding. You will need some special help." He nodded at one of his footmen, a plump frog in a buttoned-up jacket.

The frog hopped over to Rachel and Kirsty and handed them each a tiny, silver bag.

"The bags contain magic tools," the
queen told them. "Don't look inside
them yet. Open them only when
you really need to, and you will find
something to help you." She smiled at
Kirsty and Rachel.

"Look!" shouted another frog footman
suddenly. "Ruby is beginning to fade!"

Rachel and Kirsty looked at Ruby
in horror. The fairy was growing paler
before their eyes. Her beautiful dress was

no longer red, but pink, and her golden hair was turning white.

"Jack Frost's magic is still at work," said the king, looking worried. "We cannot undo his spell until the Rainbow Fairies are all together again."

"Quickly, Ruby!" urged the queen. "You must return to Rainspell at once."

Ruby, Kirsty, and Rachel rose into the air, their wings fluttering.

"Don't worry!" Kirsty called, as they flew higher. "We'll be back with all the Rainbow Fairies very soon!"

"Good luck!" called the king and queen.

Rachel and Kirsty watched Ruby worriedly as they flew off together. As they got farther away from Fairyland, Ruby's color began to return. Soon she was bright and sparkling again.

The three girls reached Rainspell at last.
Ruby led Rachel and Kirsty to the
clearing in the woods, and
they landed next to the
old, black pot. Then
Ruby scattered fairy
dust over Rachel
and Kirsty.
There was a puff
of glittering red
smoke, and the
two girls shot up
to their normal
size again.
Rachel wriggled
her shoulders. Yes,
her wings were gone.
"Oh, I really *loved*
being a fairy," Kirsty said.

They watched as Ruby sprinkled her
magic dust over the old, black pot.

"What are you doing?" Rachel asked.

"Jack Frost's magic means that I can't
help you look for my sisters," Ruby
replied sadly. "If I try, I might fade away
completely. So I will wait for you here,
in the pot at the end of the rainbow."

Suddenly, the pot began to move.
It rolled across the grass, and stopped
under the weeping willow tree. The
tree's branches hung right down to
the ground.

"The pot will be hidden under that tree," Ruby explained. "I'll be safe there."

"We'd better start looking for the other Rainbow Fairies," Rachel said to Kirsty. "Where should we start?"

Ruby shook her head. "Remember what the queen said," she told them. "The magic will come to you." She flew over and sat on the edge of the pot. Then she pushed aside one of the willow branches and waved at Rachel and Kirsty. "Good-bye, and good luck!"

"We'll be back soon, Ruby," Kirsty promised.

"We're going to find all of your Rainbow sisters," Rachel said firmly.

"Just you wait and see!"

Now it's time for Kirsty and
Rachel to help . . .

AMBER the ORANGE FAIRY.

Read on for a sneak peek . . .

A VERY UNUSUAL SHELL

"What a beautiful day!" Rachel Walker shouted, staring up at the blue sky. She and her friend Kirsty Tate were running along Rainspell Island's yellow, sandy beach. Their parents walked a little way behind them.

"It's a *magical* day," Kirsty added. The two friends smiled at each other.

Rachel and Kirsty had come to
Rainspell Island for their vacations.
But they soon found out it really *was* a
magical place!

As they ran, they passed tide pools that
sparkled like jewels in the sunshine.

Rachel spotted a little *splash!* in one of
the pools. "There's something in there,
Kirsty!" She pointed. "Let's go look."

The girls jogged over to the pool and
crouched down to see.

Kirsty's heart thumped as she gazed into the crystal-clear water. "What is it?" she asked.

Suddenly, the water rippled. A little brown crab scuttled sideways across the sandy bottom and disappeared under a rock.

Kirsty felt disappointed. "I thought it might be another Rainbow Fairy," she said.

"So did I." Rachel sighed. "Never mind. We'll keep looking."

"Of course we will," Kirsty agreed. Then she put her finger to her lips as their parents came up behind them. "*Shhh.*"

RAINBOW magic

More Titles to Read

Rainbow Fairies:
Amber the Orange Fairy

Rainbow Fairies:
Sunny the Yellow Fairy

Rainbow Fairies:
Fern the Green Fairy

Rainbow Fairies:
Sky the Blue Fairy

Rainbow Fairies:
Inky the Indigo Fairy

Rainbow Fairies:
Heather the Violet Fairy

BEHIND THE MAGIC

DAISY MEADOWS is a pseudonym for the four writers of the internationally best-selling *Rainbow Magic* series: Narinder Dhami, Sue Bentley, Linda Chapman, and Sue Mongredien. *Rainbow Magic* is the no.1 bestselling series for children ages 5 and up with over 40 million copies sold worldwide!

GEORGIE RIPPER was born in London and is a children's book illustrator known for her work on the *Rainbow Magic* series of fairy books. She won the Macmillan Prize for Picture Book Illustration in 2000 with *My Best Friend Bob* and *Little Brown Bushrat*, which she wrote and illustrated.